Smoothing over the Pudding

By Valerie Stokes-Bryant

Illustrations by Paige Valente

Acknowledgments

This is my first book. It has been in my heart for many years. I wish to dedicate it to my son, Terrence, who kept me from keeping it to myself, my daughter, Kym, who told me I could do it, to my grandson, Lucien, who is living his dream, and to my granddaughter, Maya, who sees the World in all its wonder and possibilities. To my late husband, Willie Bryant, Jr., who loved the Lord with his whole heart and me as his own flesh. With sincere gratitude to the illustrator, Paige Valente, who brought the Christian Family to life by her talent and imagination.

Credits

Contents

Chapter 1

Joyce Christian aka "See All" decided to prepare Sunday's dessert on Saturday night. As she poured the milk in the bowl to make her special pudding, her son, Thomas, aka "Be All" told his mom he wanted to help because one day he wants to be a chef like the ones he watches on TV.

"Please mom, how can I ever cook if I never try?" "You are right son" his mom said. "Wash your hands and get a large spoon."

"Ok, that's what I'm talking about," as he hurriedly did as his mother asked.

Meanwhile, Darlene Christian, aka "Do All" being the eldest of the children was looking over her science project. She called her father, Herman Christian, aka "Know All" and asked his opinion on what she had done.

"Darlene, I have never been disappointed by anything you've done," her father proudly said. "I know you always do your very best and this project is no different. I could not do any better myself and I know what I'm talking about."

Seven-year-old Jane Christian, aka "Fake All" was doing what she does best. She was in her room playing with her dolls; trying to get out of doing anything like making up her bed or picking up her toys. Jane told her mother earlier that she had a headache as she dramatically gestured toward her forehead. Jane thought no one knew she was faking, but mom sees all.

Joyce called the other children and her husband to join her and Thomas in the kitchen. "Look at this beautiful pudding Thomas and I made for Sunday's dessert." "Don't touch it!" "Ok mom, we won't," Darlene answered for everyone.

"Herman, this means you too!" Joyce said playfully to her husband.

"It is certainly going to be hard not to taste it before tomorrow, but I'll do my very best to hold out," Herman said.

Chapter 2

That night as everyone slept, Jane couldn't fall asleep. She wanted the chocolate pudding so bad she could almost taste it. She remembered what her mother said, "Don't touch it." She twist and turned in bed until she could not take it any longer. She slipped out of bed and quietly went downstairs and opened the refrigerator. In her mind she heard one voice say "don't do it, obey your mother." The other voice said, "listen to me. Get a spoon, eat some of the pudding and when you are finished smooth it over. No one will ever know you ate it." Jane ate about three heaping spoons of the tasty pudding. She smoothed it over and crept back upstairs happily to bed and fell asleep. She thought no one will ever know what she had done.

Chapter 3

T he next day after Church the family set the table and ate a wonderful dinner and anxiously anticipated dessert. As each family member passed their bowl to Joyce to give them the long awaited pudding, she proceeded to praise them for waiting. "I am so proud of each of you, yes, even you, Herman." Herman smiled and told his wife, "I know God wants me to set the example for my family, but it was not easy."

Darlene said, "Mom, I told you we would wait as you asked us to do," as she and Thomas beamed proudly. Joyce glanced at Jane, who never raised her head or looked in her direction. She seemed preoccupied as she moved her spoon back and forth in her pudding. "Jane, are you alright?" "Yes Mom, I think I have a stomach ache," as she bent over and folded her arms across her stomach as dramatic as ever. "How and when did that happen?" "You seemed to enjoy your dinner, what happened"? Jane could not take it any longer. "Mom, I am so sorry, she blurted out. "I tried to obey, but I couldn't wait, please, please, please forgive me." Joyce looked at her baby girl with love and compassion. She told her daughter she was forgiven. Jane did not have to "fake" anymore, but she did know there will be some punishment for her disobedience, and she was glad to accept it. With the forgiveness and love her mother gave her, she enjoyed this bowl of pudding much more than the pudding she ate the night before.

Now, as Joyce looked around the table she could see that all is well because she "Sees All."

The End

Smoothing over the Pudding

"IF WE REALLY WANT TO LOVE,

WE MUST LEARN HOW TO FORGIVE."

– MOTHER THERESA

"My stories intention is to mold, shape, encourage and empower children while they're young and impressionable. This valuable lesson will teach children that we are human, and we ALL make mistakes. In the truth of forgiveness, it is my hope they will grow into respectful, honest and responsible youth."

– Valerie Stokes-Bryant

KINDER CARE BOOKS

Kindercarebooks.com

Kinder 'Care' Books assists parents, teachers, caregivers, psychologists, and counselors in child psychology, morals, values, emotional, spiritual and mental health.